Nightstalker

Chapter One

Sleepwalking

It wasn't the first time Claire woke up in the woods, nor would it be the last. This marked the twentieth year it had been happening ever since she was discovered at a young age wandering out of the woods alone. She pushed her hands into the soft ground to lift her head off the pillow of cool grass beneath an oak tree.

After she sat up, she examined herself, the parts she could see. There were no marks, no bruises, and no tears in her nightgown. She dusted off the trace amounts of dirt and a couple blades of grass which attached to her hands when she placed them on the ground, but that was it. Even the soles of her feet were impeccably clean.

It was one thing to believe she suffered from a sleep walking disorder. Psychologists had been drilling it into her head from a young age. The trauma she witnessed as a child, even if most of the memories were suppressed, was locked away in the deep recesses of her mind. It didn't mean the trauma didn't exist. It was there, and it found a way to surface in the form of sleep interruptions.

All of these experts believed the sleep walking incidents would continue until that trauma was dealt with head on, until she allowed the memories to resurface. As far as she was aware, that was an impossible task. They had tried everything they could including a brief inpatient stay when she was in elementary school.

Multiple sets of foster parents couldn't handle her semi-regular nightly attempts to escape. That's how they saw what was happening. She never remembered leaving the house. All she could remember was waking up in the woods.

The doctors and therapists kept trying to fix her because they couldn't accept there was no cure. Whatever memories she might have, whatever she might have witnessed, her brain had erased it permanently. Medications didn't work. Multiple forms of therapy did little more than provide her with a place to vent. She had even reluctantly agreed to hypnosis once she became an adult, but it turned out she was part of the percentage of the population immune to being put under. She went to four different hypnotherapists before giving up. None of them could put her in a trance.

It became an accepted part of her life. This was who she was. She was a sleep walker resulting from a horrid past she would never be able to unlock.

She had been told about it. The brutality of the crime scene photographs were stored in a file in her brain. She talked to the police officers both where she was found and where she was from. All of it suggested by these experts as a way of reaching in to that hidden abyss in her mind, but to no avail.

They agreed she wouldn't be able to fully heal from the trauma until she accessed those buried memories. She believed them and agreed with it, but she had long ago accepted those memories were buried for good. None of them could explain how she could walk into the woods whether it was next door to her house or twelve miles from the foster home she lived in at the time and have clean feet when she awoke the next morning.

This morning was different. It wasn't that she was being watched. That wasn't necessarily unusual. Sometimes she was alone when she woke up, but there had been a handful of times over the years when she could feel the lingering stair of someone or something who preferred to stay hidden. It had been happening more often recently than it did when she was younger. Maybe it had always happened, but she hadn't learned to perceive the difference of when she was alone and when she could feel the presence of someone nearby.

Whatever lurked in the woods watching her didn't have four legs. It wasn't covered in fur. She'd been watched by many a small creature during hikes she took in the daylight hours. These eyes belonged to someone wholly human.

What was different this time was her arousal. Claire had never had a wet dream before, had never woke up turned on and in the mood, but she was now. It almost felt like she had been in the middle of an act which got interrupted on one level. Her body didn't have any of the physical signs. Her heart rate wasn't elevated. Her temperature hadn't risen. There was no dampness between her legs indicating foreplay, but she was excited and in dire want of sex nonetheless.

Claire scrambled to her feet and assessed her surroundings. She recognized the area from having so many visits. The trees were becoming more familiar to her than the cashiers grocery store she frequented. It wasn't far from her house. Every time she made one of these nightly treks, she always wound up in this same part of the country near where she had been found as a child. Once she gathered her bearings, she walked in the direction of home and emerged onto her property ten to fifteen minutes later. She was farther back from her house than she had expected to be on the downhill slope of the backyard where her property met the creek running through the woods.

She entered her house through the mud room off the deck and dug the package of wipes out of the storage bin where she stashed them just for this reason. The bottoms of her feet were now caked in dirt and grime from the walk home. She quickly cleaned them off before entering the main part of her pristine house.

Glancing in the kitchen on her way down the hall to the stairs, she saw the time on the microwave, 6:07 am. Her husband would've just awoke. If she was lucky, she might be able to convince him she'd never left the house.

When she opened the bedroom door, she could hear the sound of the shower running in the master bath. She opened the bathroom door and closed it softly behind her, but not quietly enough. "You're back." Her husband's voice said from behind the shower curtain.

He pulled one edge of the curtain open just enough to lean his face through and looked at her. "It always worries me what I'm supposed to do if you don't return before I have to leave for work. You always have come home, and you've always been unharmed. Still, am I to count on that?" he asked, closing the curtain again. "What if the one time I leave without actual evidence you're safe is the one time when something has happened?"

The curtain pulled back again, and his face reappeared. "And don't try to claim you were simply downstairs. I searched for you when I woke a little after three..."

Claire recoiled as though she'd been slapped. *Three in the morning? What did I do in the woods for three hours?'*

"...and saw you weren't in bed. I know you were in the woods."

She lifted her nightie off over her head, exposing her nude body.

Ian stopped talking. There would be no argument today, at least not this morning.

The curtain closed again which almost felt like a rejection, but it didn't stop her. She joined him and took the washcloth from his hand he was lathering. She washed his back for him. When her hand reached his lower back, she brought the washcloth around to his front, carefully washing him below the waist.

Ian chuckled. "You know I normally wash the rest of my body first before tending to the nether regions."

"Oh, but it's imperative to clean this area now," she said.

He spun around to face her. "Why is that?"

Claire flashed him a seductive smile. "You know how picky I am. I always wash my food before I eat it."

She dropped to her knees and took his shaft in her hands. She stroked him until he hardened. The nails on her fingers were sharp and every few strokes she'd tease them on the underside of his cock.

Claire took as much of his cock in her mouth as she could. She always told him he was too large, and her gag reflex was strong. It wasn't the full truth. She just didn't enjoy it. She didn't really enjoy any of it. Ian's member was rock hard now and she massaged it with her tongue while sliding him in and out.

She cupped his nuts and played with his balls while she sucked him off. From time to time, she'd remove his shaft from her mouth, and suck his balls into her mouth one at a time. Ian moaned and dug his fingers into her shoulders for support while she devoured him.

It would only take a few minutes. Blow jobs used to be a task she utterly despised and had to force herself to endure. A friend in college taught her a few tricks, and now she was able to get a man to cum a lot faster. Only Ian wasn't ready for this to end.

He pulled her up off the shower floor and planted a passionate kiss on her. The water sprayed down her face, and she worried briefly if she could drown while standing up. She tried to wiggle back, but his grip was firm.

When he pulled away, he turned off the water and left the shower before carefully lifting her out. He picked her up and carried her, both of them dripping wet, to the bed. He laid her on her back and parted her legs open with his own, climbing over her. There was a look in his eyes she hadn't seen before, and she enjoyed the way it made her feel. It seemed almost familiar, but no man had ever gazed at her like that until now.

There was no foreplay, not for her. He entered her as soon as he was in position. They were drenched from the shower which was all the lube they needed for him to glide inside her labyrinth swiftly.

Ian fucked her hard. He pounded into her with a fierceness he'd never shown in bed. This wasn't sex or making love; it was domination to a degree. He was showing her who she belonged to, or maybe trying to remind her. Whatever it was, it worked.

The look in his eye alone was building her to the brink. His shaft filled her completely. His was the largest cock she'd ever had. Between his size and the way he looked at her, she was able to actually cum. Her legs shook, and her body tensed. Her juices ran down his shaft while the walls of her tunnel seized hold of him, trying to keep his full length buried inside her.

When her orgasm started, Ian tensed then bucked and shot his load deep in her walls. Cumming together was a first for her, and it made her long to be able to repeat it. She knew better than to hope.

"I'm going to be late," Ian said almost as soon as he was finished. There was no cuddling after which was fine for Claire. He was the one who insisted on it, but it wasn't like him to skip it.

"Was I worth it?"

"Always." He smiled at her. He hopped off the bed and returned to the bathroom. A minute later, she heard the water turn on. He was finishing his shower.

Claire laid in bed lamenting over how it was some of the best love making she ever had. It was obviously spurred on by the arousal she felt in the woods because being sexually attracted to someone was something she never experienced. Orgasms for her were more a stroke of luck than skill. No matter what she did, she couldn't get into it.

He wasn't in the bathroom more than ten minutes before he returned freshly showered. Claire watched him as he dressed. Her husband had a fit body from working out and all the time they spent outdoors. Any woman would be lucky to make love to him, but she'd never felt that appreciation. He dressed in a hurry and left his tie draped around his neck to save a couple minutes. When he kissed her goodbye, he told her he'd grab lunch on the run since he didn't have time to make something to bring.

With his hand on the bedroom doorknob, and his back to her, he asked, "What did you do all night?"

"I don't remember," she told him softly.

Ian's stature completely changed. It was the truth, and it was the only answer she could give honestly. Sometimes she wondered if it'd be better to make something up, but the one thing she'd never be was a liar.

There would probably be a fight later because he trusted her but trust can only take you so far. That's what he told her after every one of her nightly adventures. Once he shut the door behind him, Claire sighed and rolled over to sleep. It was uncomfortable in the bed still damp from their romp, and the stress over the looming fight would hit her later. For now, she was exhausted like she always was after spending the night in the woods.

Chapter Two

Special Pills

Days after her last nocturnal stroll, Claire came home from errands to find her husband had returned from work early. It would've been a pleasant surprise, should've been. The only misgiving she should have had was she wasn't home when he arrived, but the reason for his secrecy was apparent before she even noticed his car in the driveway.

In the place where she usually parked her car was a van from Safeworks. Her husband was once again increasing their home security. The door and window alarms were standard. Almost every home had it nowadays. He once tried to add interior alarms to it, sectioning off a few rooms of the house. Their bedroom and bathroom to be specific to allow movement in those rooms after the alarms were set for the evening.

It didn't last long. If you went into the kitchen for a drink or snack in the middle of the night, the last thing on your mind was turning off the alarms before doing so. The blast of the siren when it was triggered and the calls from the security company caused both of them to wake the other one repeatedly for harmless reasons. It became more of a nuisance especially when she hadn't had a single sleepwalking episode during that time which was the entire reason he had decided to install it in the first place.

In lieu of internal alarms, he had decided to saturate their property with motion activated spotlights, thinking the lights would wake her from her episode. She would then turn around and return to bed where she belonged, next to him.

The house had been built in the country many years before either of them were born. The city was ever expanding and would probably reach them in their lifetime, but for now, it was nestled in the country, outside of the city limits, surrounded by nature. That meant all manner of four legged creatures ran through their property day and night, triggering those lights.

Ian had sprung for the best, and there was no denying the quality. Every dinner, every movie night was interrupted by the glaring shine through the windows. It made it difficult to sleep because of the light that made its way into the second story rooms as well. Claire put her foot down when he brought home room darkening curtains. This was her home too, and she had painstakingly picked out every paint color, piece of furniture, and all the décor. He wasn't ruining the ambience of their bedroom with heavy black drapes.

They had fought once before about installing outdoor security cameras which were motion activated. Claire believed she had won that fight with the help of her therapist. She didn't want them and nothing would ever change that, but she understood it may be something she'd have to agree to down the road. There had been things in her life that happened leaving a wake of consequences for her to deal with, and there were things she did want to know the answers to. Why she sleepwalked was one of them, but what she did while sleepwalking was not. The last thing she needed was humiliating video clips of her dancing on the lawn at five in the morning, maybe even performing a strip tease.

The therapist convinced her husband in a joint session it could be a detrimental blow if she wasn't ready for it, but Claire had to promise to keep an open mind about considering it for the future. The subject had never been brought up again. As she parked behind her husband's SUV and eyed the Safeworks van, she had a feeling her husband had decided to forego that conversation and ultimately risk another fight. He bit the bullet and made the decision on his own.

Claire left everything in the car. The groceries wouldn't sour by the time she made it back out to unload them. She walked into the house and followed the voices down the hall to her husband's office.

"Office," she scoffed under her breath. He needed an office no more than she needed a craft room. It was a pretense to have a space that was theirs, and theirs alone.

Someday they would have children. Claire had always wanted to have a large family mainly because family was a word as foreign to her as all the countries she'd never visited. She wanted a full litter of nine, maybe as many as twelve. Ian was far more reserved in that department. He only wanted two, a boy and a girl, as if that was something they'd be able to control. Before they married, they compromised on having four, but not for several more years to give them time for themselves first.

It was a four bedroom house, and one of those extra bedrooms was currently used by her for hobby storage. It was filled with various scrapbooking supplies, paints, beads, and other odds and ends for when Claire was struck with a creative bug. Once these four children came into the world, her crafting room would be sacrificed until the oldest two left the nest. Meanwhile, Ian's office would remain.

He didn't work from home and had no need for a home office except his desire to have it. The room wasn't exceptional. It was a desk and a computer, along with some assorted décor which Claire didn't feel fit with the design motif of the rest of the house. It was simply a room that was his and his alone. It was a place he could come to when he was upset, especially when he was upset with her, and somewhere to watch porn.

Claire didn't mind pornography, but she didn't enjoy watching it. Sex had always been a tricky subject with her. She wanted sex, enjoyed the feeling of release, but the desire had never been there. She'd never met anyone who brought it out in her. Ian could watch all the porn he wanted. The only thing that bothered her was his unnecessary need to hide it, not that he hid it well.

"And I can change the password as often as necessary?" She heard Ian ask.

"Yes," a man's voice replied. "It's really simple. Go into the settings for your account. If you have any trouble, the instructions are there in the manual, and you can always call customer service. There's twenty-four hour support."

There was some shuffling around from the other side of the closed door, and Claire could tell the technician was about to leave. "That's the screen. It will show all six camera views at one time. If you want to focus on just one, click here, and it'll pull it up. To go back to the multi-views-"

"I do this?" Ian asked.

There was no answer, so Claire assumed whatever her husband did had worked.

"They are motion activated. Right now, its set up to send a notification to your phone whenever one of the cameras detects anything. Are you sure you don't want to add another number to the account?"

"No, I'll discuss it with my wife when she gets home to see if she wants to be troubled by it all before making that decision."

'Liar,' Claire thought.

"Alright then. You have the number there. If you have any questions, just give us a call." The man's voice was closer to the door.

Claire quietly ran back to the front of the house. She walked down the hall again as though she had just arrived home. She was halfway to her husband's office when the door opened, and the technician emerged followed by Ian showing him out. "Hello," Claire smiled.

"Hi, honey," Ian said, kissing her on the cheek. "This is Brett with Safeworks. I was just showing him out." With that, the two men continued down the hall.

Claire called out to her husband. "While you're out there, would you bring in the groceries?" She heard Ian chuckle.

When the front door closed behind them, she went to the bedroom and ran the water in the master bath. Claire had just fully submerged herself in the water when her husband's voice came through the door, asking if she was okay. She didn't respond.

The door knob jiggled as he tried to come in, and she smirked. They never locked the door when they were in the tub or shower to allow the other one the opportunity to join them. She pictured the look of shock on his face and splashed the water on her arms.

"I can hear the water, so I guess that means you're still alive in there."

Claire rolled her eyes. How could he be so calm? He knew damn well and good installing those cameras was going to piss her off. How could he act so nonchalant?

"Well, I guess you had a bad day."

'Are you kidding me? Is he baiting me? He must be trying to instigate a fight.'

"I'll put everything away. What would you like for dinner?"

When she didn't answer, he asked, "How does Chinese sound?"

She continued to bathe and ignored him.

"I'll take your silence as agreement then."

Claire finally heard his footsteps move away from the door, leaving her in peace. She sank into the water, resting her head on the edge of the tub and closed her eyes. Maybe she had jumped the gun by running away from him so quickly today. It was going to create triple the amount of work for her by not putting groceries away herself. They had lived in this house for two years, and he still didn't know where anything went. She'd spend the better part of the next day and a half hunting down everything she just purchased from wherever he stashed it. Then she'd have to put it away where it belonged.

When she finally left the bathtub, she went straight to bed. It was an hour before dinner, but she didn't care. From her purse, she pulled out the bottle of sleeping pills. They were jokingly referred to as special pills by her and Ian. They worked a little too well. These pills would knock her out cold for hours, but she felt hungover the next morning. It would take half a day to recover.

When they were first prescribed, she took them every night, but it didn't take long to develop a tolerance. The pills worked great for about a week. Then they'd only put her to sleep for a short period of time. She'd be wide awake and full of energy for several hours. It'd be around time for Ian to wake up before she was finally tired enough to sleep again.

She used them for special occasions. The thought always made her laugh. Sleeping pills for those events you don't want to miss. When they'd travel, she'd take them. Whenever she had a night time event as doctors called it, she'd wake in the same area of the woods. If she had a sleepwalking occurrence while out of state, or worse, out of the country, she didn't want to think about what might happen to her while trying to get back to those woods. Maybe she'd finally go somewhere else. It was a chance she wasn't going to take.

Claire didn't take one right away, but she set the bottle on the nightstand to make Ian believe she had. It was going to be a long night, but it was worth it. She'd pretend to be asleep whenever he came into the room. Long after he went to bed, she'd silence his phone then go outside and trigger the cameras to record, giving him the show he so desperately wanted. She would make a fool of herself out there until she felt like he had enough video to satisfy his need to be right and cause one of their worst fights to date. She'd take the pill before actually going to sleep, so she'd be dead to the world when he got ready for work instead of dealing with his bullshit.

Chapter Three

His House

The next few days were tense. They barely spoke to each other except when absolutely necessary. Claire continued to ignore him most of the time while Ian acted like the brunt of the problem must be on her shoulders. She had a bad day. Something was bothering her as if he didn't know damn well and good what it was that pissed her off. The little dance she did on the lawn the night after the cameras were installed had never been mentioned. Ian probably thought it was real, and this was his wife when she sleep walked.

It finally came to a head, and they exploded. Ian defended his decision to get the cameras. Yes, he had agreed to give her time, but it was becoming obvious the additional security was something she was never going to give honest consideration. This was his house. *'It was their house.'* She was his wife, and it was his duty to protect her. He was fully in his right to do everything necessary, and that included motion activated cameras.

Claire's stance was the humiliation she'd endure. He wasn't even going to let her see the images on the video which he claimed wasn't true. Then why not give her the access while the technician was here to set it up? She wanted more control over it, to make sure no one saw her on camera except for Ian. That set off a new string of fights about how she didn't trust him.

They spent all of today staying out of each other's way until dinner. Ian called a truce, and Claire went along with it. She was still angry with him. That wasn't going away anytime soon, but she was exhausted from maintaining it.

When they went to bed, she allowed Ian access to her body as a sign the fight was behind them. She wasn't feeling it tonight, not that she ever did, but tonight she really wasn't in it more than usual.

It was the most cordial sex she'd ever had in her life. Need me here? Yes, sir. Here you go. Want more of that? Happy to oblige. Let me just move a little out of your way. Is that better? Anything for you dear.

This wasn't exactly what was being said, but it might as well have been. On her end, there was nothing. No excitement, no build up, no passion, and certainly no orgasms. It was a lot of work for her to fake one, and it took even more effort to use Ian's lovemaking to bring herself to a real one although it could be done.

She wasn't into it tonight. It didn't help that she was so tired. She just didn't have the energy to be a more active participant. She didn't just lay there, but she squeaked by with minimal effort. She went through the motions of what Ian liked with an occasional moan when it occurred to her to do so to urge him on.

Ian never noticed, nor did she expect anything different from him. He was in his own zone of trying to be a sex god, which he was not, and wasn't distracted by whether or not his wife was getting hers out of it. Usually, she longed for more time with him, for him to last just a couple minutes more. She could bring herself to an orgasm, but not if he came too soon.

Tonight would've been perfect for it because she thought he'd never finish.

When he rolled off her, he told her it was the best sex they ever had, and she could tell by the look in his eyes he meant it. Claire turned away, so he couldn't see her smile. It was all she could do not to laugh. His best night of sex, and all she did was give him her body to use like a masturbation tool. Of course, he thought it was awesome. There were none of her own likes and dislikes getting in the way of his satisfaction.

After laying in the afterglow, his afterglow, for no more than a minute, she threw the covers back and sat up. Ian was spent and would be out soon. She could've waited until he was asleep, but she wanted him to know how unsatisfied she was by how easily she walked and the normal sound of her breathing. Normally, she was the queen of faking orgasms, but she was still pissed at him.

"Where are you going?" His voice was strained from being out of breath.

"Don't worry," she sighed. "I'm only headed to the kitchen. My throat's a little sore."

'Not from moaning in response to anything you did.'

"Gonna make some tea with honey. Want anything?" She painted a smile on her face like nothing was out of sorts.

"Nah," he said. "Hurry back."

She walked down the stairs, but bypassed the kitchen. Instead, she turned down the hall to the door of his office. It was locked. Claire rolled her eyes. It was rare when he did this and usually meant one of two things. There was either porn in there he didn't want her to see, or he was flirting with a new intern at work. This time she suspected it was because of the cameras.

He didn't want her snooping and figuring out how to mess with them.

The key was in his pocket, but she made a copy of it not long after they moved into the house. She kept her spare office key in the junk drawer. He'd have seen it by now if he knew where to find the scissors without having to ask his wife. She fished it out and unlocked the door.

Claire walked into the office and sat at the desk. There was a cigar box that had belonged to Ian's father, but Ian didn't smoke. She lifted the lid and moved a few odds and ends around until she found it. At the bottom of the box was a folded piece of paper containing all of Ian's log on's and passwords. He couldn't remember them, so he kept them in the most obvious place anyone would look, like an idiot.

She logged onto his computer. There was a time when the insecure woman inside her would take the opportunity to snoop through everything, but she was drained from the last round of fights. She'd welcome another woman challenging her for Ian and might even willingly let him go if she could keep the house.

From the favorites tab, she pulled up the sign in page of Safeworks. It was pretty easy to figure out from there. Claire checked under his account and settings until she found where she could disable the cameras. Once they were off, she logged out of everything and made sure nothing had been moved on the desk. Ian was an obsessive nut over things like that, but not anything else. He could tell if she moved a picture frame a quarter of an inch on the mantel while dusting.

If it was behind a closed door, he was lost. Out of sight, out of mind. He still didn't know which cabinet had the coffee mugs and in which drawer she kept the scissors. The pantry was like a maze he couldn't solve. Send him to grab the pasta, and he'd come back with quart sized baggies, a bag of chocolate chips, and microwavable popcorn claiming he couldn't find anything else.

When she went back to bed, she slept well for the first time in almost a week. It was a peaceful feeling to know you weren't being monitored. In the morning, she'd have to remember to go back downstairs and turn the cameras on again. Ian would figure out what she was up to eventually, probably with her next episode, but she wanted to stick with it as long as she could.

She woke up five minutes before his alarm and quickly snuck downstairs, using the bathroom located off the kitchen instead of the master. After turning the cameras on, she went into the kitchen to make a pot of coffee. That's where Ian found her a few minutes later.

"When you weren't in bed," he began.

"You thought I was off gallivanting." Claire finished the statement for him.

Ian shook his head and headed to the stairs. "Please don't. Not today. Certainly not this early."

"But am I wrong? Did you for one second think I was in the kitchen preparing to start breakfast?"

He didn't answer her.

"Exactly. If I'm not in *your* bed, I'm up to no good."

"I have to shower," he said, taking the steps two at a time.

This is what she'd have to do every night until he figured it out, even after he figured it out for that matter. The password was her name followed by the month and day of their anniversary. She'd tell him she simply guessed it. She'd keep it up as long as she could and hope he didn't realize how easily she found his passwords.

Without any memory of her episodes, she had no idea if there will ever be anything embarrassing on the videos. She always woke up in her nightgown in the woods, but there's a lot of time left unaccounted.

If she does do something extreme, like strip on the lawn, at least she puts her clothes back on. She doesn't know what she's doing when she's walking around, one foot in real life and the other in a different world. If she's walking around talking to people who aren't there or mimicking actions, it would be embarrassing to see it. That's something she'd been told can be done during sleep walking episodes. Maybe she's on the lawn pushing a cart because she thinks she's at the grocery store doing the shopping. If that's the case, she doesn't want video proof of any of it.

Ian said he'll never do anything with it. She trusts he'd never post it online or do anything publicly humiliating with it like that. She even half believes he won't share the videos with other people, but she's not convinced he won't show his mom or his sister. She could see him asking someone close to him for advice on what to do. That alone would humiliate her whenever she was around those people again. It would always be at the front of her mind that they know.

Her biggest fear was he would use it against her in her therapy. He would bring his evidence to future joint sessions and use it to force her into more intensive therapy which she didn't want.

Chapter Four

Bedtime

Claire looked out the windows of the family room in the back of the house at the woods that stretched along their property line. Ian had gone to bed early, but she was nowhere near tired. He hated it. He hated when she didn't turn in at the same time as he did. This wasn't the 1950's. A man wasn't supposed to make the decisions for his wife even if she was beginning to feel like she might need the help. Still, she wouldn't be too long. There was no need in causing a senseless argument with all the real issues they had been dealing with.

What Claire really needed was a few minutes alone with the trees. They calmed her, cleared her mind. They always had. People who didn't know assumed she was a natural outdoorsy type. Maybe that's all it was. Maybe the woods would've always held an attraction for her. She knew better. She knew it stemmed from her childhood, from where she had been found, and from the memories she couldn't access.

Her therapy session that afternoon had not gone well. She expected her therapist to be on her side, to encourage her to take a stand against Ian. She had hoped her therapist would suggest another joint session where the therapist could explain to Ian how detrimental these cameras were to her recovery since Ian wouldn't listen to his own wife. Instead, the traitor sided with her husband. *It was time.*

The cameras are already installed.

Give them a chance.

If it had truly bothered you, why didn't you call before now?

"I didn't call because I had an appointment scheduled two days later," she said to the windows.

She wanted to take a walk in the woods, but she didn't dare. If she left right now, the cameras would alert Ian. He would be downstairs before she made it to the tree line. If she turned off the cameras and went for a walk, it would be risky. It was rare, but sometimes when she didn't go to bed right away, he'd come down to see what she was doing. With her luck, tonight would be one of those nights.

It infuriated her the way he didn't trust her. He claimed he did, but actions speak louder than words. His actions said he didn't.

Claire never did anything except run errands, take care of the house, and study a couple classes a semester to work toward her Master's Degree. It was a degree he didn't think she needed. There was no need for her to continue her education anyway. When they had children, he didn't want her to work.

Career or no career, she wanted the education. Their compromise was she would take classes online. He claimed he didn't want her to be overstressed, triggering more issues with her therapy. The truth was he didn't want her around a bunch of single, young men who might catch her eye, not because of their looks, but because they didn't try to keep her under constant surveillance.

"It's not that bad." She sighed and walked down the hall to his office, turning off the cameras before going to bed. Whenever she and Ian fought, her mind always grasped at all the worst pieces of their relationship, ignoring all the good.

When she walked in the bedroom, she found not only was Ian still awake, but he was sitting up in bed, looking over a file for a big court case he had in the morning. She had been right not to risk a walk outside. He was waiting for her. The way he smiled when she walked in the room clearly said what he wanted.

'Why doesn't he just say so?'

Whenever Ian said he was going to bed early, it was hard to tell what was on his mind. Some nights he wanted sex. Some nights he was upset about something, usually something involving her, and he wanted a few minutes to escape and unwind. Other nights he was actually tired.

It bewildered her how difficult it was for him to communicate this. Just give her a kiss, nibble her ear, and say, "Let's go to bed, so I can devour your body."

Or, "I'm really stressed. I need a few minutes alone. I need a little bit more downtime to unwind before I can fall asleep."

Maybe, "I'm exhausted, so I'm going to bed early."

Claire smiled at him and lifted her nightgown off over her head before climbing into bed. This would be good for her too. Even though she didn't necessarily enjoy sex, orgasms had a universal effect. They were nature's best stress relief. A few more nights like this, and she probably wouldn't be upset about the new routine, having to remember to turn off the surveillance cameras before bed.

He melted into her and began kissing her before she was fully on the bed. The heat emanating off his body was immense. He hugged her to him, enjoying the feel of her, the scent of her, and the passion with which she was kissing him.

It was hopeless. Claire's body didn't react in the way

Hollywood had always described it should.

'Best to get it over with now that it's started.' She snaked a hand down and rubbed his erection through his pajama bottoms and murmured, "I want you."

She reached her hand inside the waistline and grasped his burgeoning erection. She slipped the head of his cock in her mouth, taking it in until it hit the back of her throat.

"You don't have to do that," he coaxed. He lifted her up and kissed her then laid her on the bed.

Ian moved over top of her and wet two fingers to moisten her tunnel. He leveled his cock down to enter her, then pushed into her snug, warm labyrinth until he was all the way in. He rocked forward till the base of his abdomen was pressed against her clit.

"Oh, that feels so good." Claire said the words more from repetition and memory then anything.

"Play with your breasts," Ian ordered. "Wet your fingers, and play with your nipples."

This was new. He usually didn't offer instructions. It's either porn or a new intern. She did as he asked. "Oh, faster... Oh, yes! Yes!" The words always felt silly coming out of her mouth, but she learned long ago men like to hear them.

He stroked her with fast controlled thrusts, relishing the feel of her hot, slippery tunnel. She was now squeezing, rolling and pinching her fat nipples and nodding her head as if she approached climax. He leaned forward over her so he could ratchet his hips faster.

It was feeling pretty good, and she slipped one of her hands to her clit to encourage a climax. Ian was trying hard to please her tonight, so she wanted to help him out.

"Oh, oh fuck, Ian! Oh, yes, fuck me." The words trickled out, and she tried to make eye contact while reciting them. He was looking down, watching his thrusts in and out.

She released her breast and grabbed his ass with one hand, arching her back off the bed. It was a universal sign for sexual enjoyment she had learned about in college and had used it ever since to help make her fake orgasms seem real, but she was close this time. It could still happen.

Ian bucked into her harder and deeper with each stroke. His climax was getting closer.

Claire rubbed her clit vigorously, hoping to reach hers too. While she didn't feel the attraction and passionate hunger others raved about, she did experience every drop of frustration from not cumming. There wasn't enough time. She wouldn't reach hers before he shot his load.

She dropped back on the bed, letting her back relax. Ian would take it as a sign her orgasm had peaked, and it was now safe to release his wad. She closed her eyes, and the woods flashed behind her lids. That one spot beneath the oak tree where she always returned. She could see it as clearly as if she were there, but only for one moment. And, she could feel the stare upon her like she was being watched.

Her body shuddered as her climax surged through her. "Oh, fuck! I'm cumming!" She cried out, but it wasn't fake this time.

It was all Ian could take. He unloaded, cumming hard inside his wife, thrusting rapid fire as his own orgasm blasted through him. He reached the end and bucked violently a couple times before collapsing on top of her, still not looking at her.

'Intern,' Claire decided.

After a few ragged breaths, he carefully moved over and lay

on his side next to her. "Wow," he muttered.

"Wow?"

"After all this time, sex with you keeps getting better and better."

'It helps having a real life fantasy driving you.' Claire realized both of them were guilty in that aspect. Something drew her to the woods, and though she didn't know what it was, she suspected it had something to do with her sexual malfunctioning.

'Maybe if they had sex in the woods?' No. That was her special place. She wasn't about to spoil it by tainting it with a cheating, controlling husband even if she made the choice long ago to stay with him through it all. No one else would want her with her history, sleepwalking, and sexual malfunctions.

The sound of snoring hit her ears, and she glanced at Ian. He was already out. It was something she envied about men. They could fall asleep in an instant while she tossed and turned for what could take hours.

Claire slipped out of bed and cleaned herself up in the bathroom. When she laid back down, she thought about the woods and wondered why it popped into her mind at that moment. It never had before tonight. It could've been coincidence, but she felt it was more than that. The call she felt to the woods had been growing stronger recently. There had to be a connection. She drifted off still trying to figure it out.

When she awoke the next morning, she could feel the woods around her before she opened her eyes and her senses kicked in to action. There was the unmistakable sensation of being watched. Then she felt the cool grass underneath her and heard the birds singing to each other in the trees.

Claire smiled with her eyes still closed imagining the tales they were spreading. In her mind, she pictured the birds letting everyone know the beautiful stranger had awakened. *'Beautiful?'* She opened her eyes and saw the rays of light softly streaming through the upper branches of the trees. *'Where did that come from?'*

It wasn't a word she typically used when describing herself, but she had those good days when she felt it. She was attractive and pretty, yes, but beautiful wasn't a compliment she accepted easily.

Then she became aware of the rest of the sensations thrust upon her body as she stirred. There was a definitive wetness between her legs. She hadn't had a cycle for over two years thanks to the birth control she was on, so it wasn't that. When she began to stand, her legs trembled. Claire sat back down for a moment confused by her own body. *'Did I orgasm out here last night?'*

The thought terrified her. If she had, she would convince herself it was caused by her own hand. Literally. It would always lurk in the back of her mind however. What if?

'No. No, I didn't,' she realized. There was another feeling she wasn't used to. It was something foreign to her, but a slow realization came over her as she figured it out. She was horny.

Claire forced her legs to work. Her steps wobbled for the first few feet before becoming stronger. Once she was able, she ran to the house, hoping to get inside before Ian woke up, or at the very least before he discovered she was gone.

Chapter Five

Breakfast

Claire ran in the back door and didn't bother stopping in the mud room to clean her feet when she came inside hoping to save time. The clock on the microwave told her she had fifteen minutes until Ian's alarm went off. She went back to the mud room and cleaned herself up. Then she placed two of the wipes on the floor under her feet, shimmying down the hallway to wipe up any tracks she might have left. There was nothing visible to her eye, but there's no telling what Ian might discern when he came downstairs.

By the time she finished, her breathing had returned to normal, and it wasn't as evident she had just raced the clock to get home without being found out. She stood in the kitchen filling the carafe for a pot of coffee. The ache between her legs was still prevalent.

This sensation was foreign to her. She's never known what it felt like to crave sex, to long for her pussy to be crammed full of cock, to be in desperate need of release. The only time she's come close was at the end of sex when she was unable to orgasm. Then and only then had she felt the need for climax was when her body had been taken to the brink and denied. She fumbled with the coffee filters as her body betrayed her. Both legs were weak from the lust coursing through her veins and the sprint so soon after waking up.

Once the pot was brewing, she turned her attention to breakfast. It'd have to be something quick and easy this morning. There was no way she trusted herself to cook in her present condition. She opened the refrigerator doors, scanning her options, and glanced at the counters. Bagels and cream cheese spread it was. She set the tub on the counter and was untying the plastic bag of bagels when Ian's voice caused her to jump.

"You better be careful," he said, sounding almost angry.

'Shit! I've been busted.'

Claire faced him only to find a twinkling in his eye. He was joking about something without realizing how spot on it actually was. "Why's that?" Claire smiled at him, walking over to greet him with a kiss.

"Because I could get used to this," he said, bringing his lips to hers.

"Used to what?" Claire asked when she pulled away.

"Breakfast." Ian laughed and swatted her ass.

She squinted at him and shook her head. "I almost always cook you breakfast."

"Yes, but not until after your first cup of coffee which I bring to you in bed."

Claire laughed because it was the truth. She did need the first cup of caffeine energizing her system before she could trust herself to operate anything in the kitchen. A morning run, she learned, would wake her up just as fast.

She went back to the bag of bagels, and Ian stood next to her removing two coffee mugs from the cabinet. The scent of him was so close, and it quickened the pulse she felt throb in her clit. He hadn't showered yet, so his scent was musky, remnants of last night's sex and sweat from his sleep. If you had described the aroma to her yesterday, she would have recoiled as her stomach turned. This morning it hit the spot and made her want him.

'I want him.' Claire was bewildered. *'I have never wanted anyone. Ever.'*

Claire sliced a bagel in half and slipped it into the slots on the larger side of the toaster. They hardly ever used the other side for regular bread anymore. She had to concentrate on each movement until completion because her mind was consumed with desire.

Ian noticed the weird expression on his wife's face and asked what was wrong. She looked at him. Her expression unchanging, and then she pounced.

Before Ian could react, his pajama bottoms lay in a heap on the floor, and his wife was crouched in front of him. He gently tugged at her shoulders to lift her up to him, but she refused to be budged. "Honey," he soothed. "I can't be late again."

Claire moaned as she freed Ian's hard cock from his boxers. He was saying one thing, but his member was begging to be sucked. The head of his dick pointed right at her, exciting her.

"Honey," he said again, trying to get her attention.

She wrapped one hand around his shaft, gobbling it in her mouth, wetting every last inch of his cock, while her free hand dipped beneath her nightgown in between her legs.

"Claire." He said her name loudly, but there was a moan in his voice that came out with it. He wanted it too. Ian gave in to his wife's demanding actions and placed his hands on her head, pushing his fingers into her hair.

She smiled at her victory and paused to take a deep breath. She gave the base of his shaft a gentle squeeze before stroking it a few times, admiring it. Everything looked and felt different to her now like she was experiencing sex for the first time.

Ian's cock jerked under her touch. The warmth and lightness of her grip was exquisite. His wife's entire focus was on his throbbing member. She licked her lips and slowly leaned her head back in toward him. He'd never seen her go down on him with such intensity.

"Oh, fuck!" Ian groaned when he felt his wife's breath on him. His shaft jerked in her hand which made Claire moan.

Claire teased the tip with her tongue, running it around the head of his cock. She flicked it slowly before rolling her eyes up in her head, moaning as she did. Instead of taking him fully in her mouth again, she couldn't resist one last tease. She licked the head once more, lingering on the tip with her tongue while stroking the base of his shaft.

Her husband watched through gritted teeth while Claire played with him. Her hand tightened and loosened its grip on him while she stroke his cock. The arousal was heavenly. His shaft was pulsating, displaying his eagerness. Claire seemed like she was in complete control while his breathing was rapid and shallow. He couldn't stand it any longer. "Fuck, Claire! Suck me, now!"

She heard the bagel pop up in the toaster like a timer had gone off. It acted as her cue. She wrapped her lips around the head of his rock hard cock. Her mouth tightened around him and she worked her tongue along the tip as well.

Ian threw his head back and gasped. His wife did this so well, but today was new. This was different, and it was better which he hadn't thought possible. He gripped her head tighter, not trying to force it down on him. Claire didn't like it, so he resisted the almost natural urge.

Claire sucked more of him into her mouth. She went down and inch then came back to the head. When she brought him into her mouth again, she'd go a little farther each time. In a minute, her lips touched his abdomen at the base of the shaft.

"Fuuuuccckkk," he groaned loudly.

She bobbed her head up and down, violently sucking his cock. Her eagerness surprised even herself.

He dropped his gaze to the top of her head, watching as she worked. "That feels amazing," he muttered between broken breaths. It'd be over soon at this rate which he didn't want. When Claire pulled her head back for another deep breath, he made his move. He bent down and lifted her under her shoulders. When he had her half on her feet which was difficult because she wanted to stay where she was, he turned her around and leaned her against the island in the kitchen. He slid her legs apart and stood between them. His cock throbbed against the thin material of her nightgown that covered her ass.

Ian leaned up and kissed her neck, trailing the kisses over her shoulder and down her back. He continued until he dropped to his knees behind her, sliding her nightgown up over her round ass. His cock bounced while he stared at it approving of what his eyes saw.

He caressed her ass with his hands and took in her aroused scent. Claire's juices were already dripping between her legs, and he gently lapped them up on both her inner thighs.

Claire moaned and gripped the far side of the island for support. At her height, she had to stand on her tip toes to bend over it.

"Wider!" Ian demanded. "Spread those legs."

She stepped her feet apart more, but Ian pushed them

farther. He squeezed the cheek of her ass, and she felt the ache inside her grow stronger. It wouldn't take much to make her cum. She wasn't sure that she wouldn't while he played with her ass.

Ian buried his face into her pussy and touched his tongue to her. He ran his tongue along her lips, parting them slightly, he groaned and lapped again. This time he forced his tongue into her entrance slightly while spreading her ass cheeks with both hands.

A steady stream of moans escaped Claire's mouth as he began to eat her pussy more forcefully. His tongue slipped inside, scooping up her wetness before he moved just enough to change the position of his head to find her clit too. He rubbed it with the tip of his tongue. Claire was practically off the floor now, laying with her torso sprawled over the island which helped him bury his face in her spread thighs even from behind.

"Yes! Oh God, yes!" Claire cried out, feeling the pleasure grow with each passing second. His tongue slid in and out, running and flicking over her clit. Her knuckles turned white as her grip tightened. She was growing closer and closer to orgasm.

Hearing her pleasured moans was music to Ian's ears. He savored the sounds almost as much as he savored the scent and taste of her pussy. He pushed his tongue as deep as he could inside her to suckle the sweet and sticky juices he knew he'd find. Something was different this morning. The thought nagged his mind, but he was going to enjoy it.

"Damn! That feels so good!" Claire groaned and her legs shuddered. Ian took her clit between his lips, sucking it before returning to her labyrinth. It wouldn't be much longer, and she wasn't even going to have to work toward it.

Her juice poured out of her and soaked his face. He eagerly lapped at her clit then pulled away for a deep breath. "You're so damn delicious," he moaned, licking his lips. He lined up her box, staring at the display right before his eyes before attacking it again. He buried his face between her open thighs, and shoved his tongue into her warm, wet opening.

While he worked her tunnel, he squeezed and massaged her ass cheeks. He explored her depths, returning to the hidden areas of pleasure he'd discovered years ago. The ultimate reward of her sweet juices spilled over his taste buds as he brought her closer. His cock throbbed, mirroring the pleasure he felt.

Claire's moans became louder and more ragged as Ian licked her pussy with renewed gusto. He wiggled and flicked his tongue deep inside her inner passage before pulling out and focusing on her clit. He rubbed her nub, sending shockwaves through Claire's body. Her legs shook with pleasure as she held onto the edge of the island for support.

"Oh, fuck! Yes!" The words cried out of her freely as his tongue slipped back into her tunnel. He let go of her ass and reached around her leg to find and rub her pulsating clit, adding a new level of stimulation. Her orgasm rocked through her body, and she held onto the island for dear life as her legs betrayed her, shaking uncontrollably.

Chapter Six

Always on My Mind

Without a word, Ian pulled his face from his wife's wet mound, feeling the juices sticking to his skin. He licked his lips and gave an appreciative moan at the taste. His nostrils were filled with her scent, and his cock stiffened to an almost painful response when he stood up.

"Oh, fuck," Claire groaned as the last few waves of her orgasm subsided. She was on fire and desperate to be filled by Ian's member. Luckily, she didn't have to wait long.

He looked down at her, bent over the island. Her ass was in the air looking good enough to eat. Her skin flushed and the slight sheen of sweat caused it to glisten. It was so arousing. Seeing her like this alone would've driven him wild even without the buildup they already had.

"It's time to burn off those calories from breakfast," Ian joked. He stepped behind Claire and guided his cock to her entrance. He pressed the tip to her, shuddering as he felt her heat envelop him and pushed inside with a thrust of his hips.

"Oh, yes! Fuck me, Ian!" Claire tilted her head back and let out a loud cry of pleasure as she was stretched by his cock thrusting into her. The feeling of him filling her, his shaft sliding inside inch by inch as the head forced its way deep caused her to lose all control over her volume. The desire, the need was a new experience, and she let it take her over.

Ian drew out a groan of his own as he felt the velvety wetness of his wife's labyrinth massage his cock which jerked and throbbed inside her. He'd felt it many times since their first time together, but that morning in their kitchen with Claire bent over the island, it felt extra good, almost like it was tighter and softer than normal, and her inner walls squeezed harder burying his shaft deeper.

Placing his hands on her hips, he slid backwards and pulled his cock out until only the head was nestled in her folds. He thrust forward again, driving his full length into her with a firm roughness, making her body shake and pressing her breasts hard onto the counter top.

"Oh, God! Yes... Yes!" Claire moaned in ragged breathless gasps as Ian began fucking her, slamming hard in and out of her from behind. She helplessly held onto the edge of the island with white knuckled intensity as Ian, fueled by his own intense need and primal desires, drove himself deep over and over.

His cock throbbed as it slid easily into the dripping wet passage that was his wife's tunnel in full blown excitement. Every time he thrust forward and slammed the head as deep as he could, a loud slap of his body hitting her ass rang out. It added to the symphony of moans and grunts accompanying them. There was no love making this morning. This was pure unadulterated fucking.

"Fuck! I'm gonna cum!" Claire gasped as she felt Ian's cock again driving into her. His shaft stretched her inner walls for a second as the entire length was forced into her deep before he pulled out again. The sensation of emptiness lasting only long enough to be noticed before he drove himself inside her again.

Ian could hardly hear her words. He was too lost in the

pleasure as he fucked her tight, wet pussy, but he could feel the tell-tale signs of her impending orgasm. Feeling those only made him want to fuck her harder. His cock stiffened again as he drove it deep.

"Yes! Fuck! Fuck! Yes!" Claire cried. She was completely lost in pure orgasmic delight as she felt Ian's hands pull her hips back to meet his forward thrusts now. The sounds of their bodies slamming together loud and clear in the kitchen, and the feel of her sweat on the island underneath her as she was fucked on top of it. The movement of her body being pulled and pushed by the force of Ian's thrusts into her passage caused Claire's nipples to rub against the hard counter. The sensitive, rock hard, pink nubs sent waves of pleasure coursing through her, adding to the already mind blowing delights of being thoroughly fucked.

Ian grunted as he slammed his cock again and again into Claire as she rushed towards a huge climax. He couldn't help but throw his head back as he felt the surge of heat and wetness that preceded her orgasm. Her juices flowed and coated his shaft as well as ran down her inner thighs.

"Oh yeah, cum for me baby, cum for me!" Ian growled as he drove his pulsing cock deep with a rough thrust of his hips, and pulled her backward to meet him at the same time, forcing himself fully inside her dripping pussy which suddenly tightened around him as her orgasm erupted.

Claire's body tensed, and her legs began to shake as the pleasure suddenly exploded inside her. She couldn't speak. She could only let out a series of gasps and squeals while the climax rocked through her. Her hand clenched on the edge of the counter for support. It was all that held her in place as she felt his cock throb inside her convulsing tunnel.

Ian groaned as the ripples of Claire's climax traveled over his shaft. It was much more intense this time than he could ever remember it being, and it was driving him crazy. His cock felt like it was nestled inside a velvet vice when she squeezed his length. He couldn't take if for much longer, and he slid back to thrust deep, starting to fuck her hard and fast.

In her mind, she was screaming for him to fuck her harder, to give her more, but she was too out of breath to make the words form outside her own head. Ian's cock slid out of her only to be driven hard back inside as his weight slammed into her, making another orgasm brew as soon as her previous one began to subside.

Ian reached forward and grabbed her hair in his right hand, holding it tightly and tilting her head back farther. They had reached new heights together this morning, and he only wished he could see her face, see the pleasure revealed on it he was giving her.

Feeling him grab her long hair added to her arousal. "Yes!" Claire cried out. She slid her feet a little wider on the tile floor as much to steady herself as to give Ian better access. Her thighs still trembled and quivered from her orgasm.

Ian felt her movement and took advantage of it. He pulled back on Claire's hair, using it as leverage to drive his hips forward and slam his rock hard cock deep into her. He was rewarded with another cry of pleasure and a fresh coating of her juices all over his shaft.

"Damn! You're hotter than hell," he groaned. He gave her a long slow thrust enjoying the sensation of her labyrinth swallowing him inch by inch before he began again with a renewed pace. Their bodies slapped together so often like they were applauding each other.

Claire squealed feeling another orgasm building quickly. Every thrust pushed her closer to the peak. The tightness in his voice when he spoke told her he was on the verge of losing control too.

"I'm close," Ian moaned. His thrust became more unpredictable as he neared the brink. His cock jerked inside her more frequently, and his balls tightened preparing to release his load.

"Oh, God!" Claire was filled with excitement trying to hold back her own release to time it with Ian's. It wasn't easy. She was on fire, and her clit radiated waves of pleasure that were almost too much to withstand.

Ian gave a few final thrusts before he couldn't hold back any longer. He drove his shaft deep, and his body collapsed on top of his wife. His cock pulsed. The first spurt of his cum sprayed from the tip, filling her. As he began to release, Claire let go and let her climax wash over him as well. Both of them breathed in ragged, gasping breaths as their bodies shook in unison. The indescribable joys of their orgasms rippled between each other in a shared moment of pleasure.

Claire continued to moan as a second and third jet of cum was shot into her. Ian's cock jerked each time it released more into her eagerly accepting tunnel. She was thankful she was bent over the island at that moment because it was holding her up. Her legs alone wouldn't be able to support her.

When he was finally spent, Ian rested on top of her. He enjoyed the heat of her body against his while he recovered some of his strength. His head spun and felt light after such an intense climax, and his body sheened with sweat.

"Now, the worst part," Ian said, kissing Claire on the cheek. He pushed himself off her, sliding his cock out of her dripping passage. "Cleaning up."

Claire giggled because she had been thinking the same thing. There would be added work for her to do today in the kitchen. She remained on the island a few more minutes, but she shifted positions to prop herself up more as the last shockwaves of her orgasm decreased their intensity while traveling through her body.

"I'm going to be late," Ian said. He was smiling at least when the words came out of his mouth.

"Did you like your breakfast?" Claire teased.

Ian shot her a playful look and shook his head. "What am I going to do with you?"

Claire pushed away from the island but kept her hands gripped to the edge for support while she tested how well her legs could hold up. "I have a few ideas."

"Breakfast," Ian said slowly, "was delicious." He leaned over the other side of the island and gave her a deep lingering kiss. "But I really do need to shower now and get ready for work."

"Glad you enjoyed it," Claire said with a smirk. "It took a lot out of me making it."

Ian gazed at her for a moment then headed for the stairs. When he reached them, he stopped and asked, "What's got into you?"

"What do you mean?"

"You've never been so wild before, Claire. You've been holding out on me." He was grinning ear to ear when he took the stairs two at a time to their bedroom.

Claire was exhausted and considered going straight to sleep, but the nagging worry came back about Ian discovering where she'd been. She'd wait until after he left and decided to give areas of the kitchen a wipe down. Easier to do it now than later. When she was through, she headed toward the stairs, but luckily glanced back down the hall for any tracks she might've missed when she first came home. As soon as she saw his office door, she realized she hadn't even turned the cameras back on yet. She took advantage of his absence to get it done. It didn't seem likely he'd check this morning since he was already late, but she didn't want to forget about it either.

When she made it to their room, Ian was ready to run out the door. "I half expected to find you nestled up in bed asleep when I got out of the shower." He kissed her again before tying his tie.

"I cleaned up downstairs first."

"You know, it's okay to leave a mess for a little bit," he laughed.

Claire shrugged and stood between the bed and the bathroom trying to talk herself into a shower before laying down, but she had very little energy left.

Ian came up behind her, gripping her upper arms. He kissed her neck and whispered in her ear. "I won't be able to stop thinking about you today." Then he was gone.

It made her smile, but only briefly. She looked out the bedroom window on the back side of the house and stared at the woods. There was something she wouldn't be able to get off her mind either, but unfortunately, it wasn't her husband.

Chapter Seven

Security Issues

It happened at least a half dozen more times. Claire would awake in the woods with lust raging through her body and come home to take it out on Ian. The rest of the time, their sex life was lackluster. More of the same. She could take it or leave it, but wanted to please her husband. That's what she tried to do.

She should've known her luck would run out. It didn't take long before the technician was out at the house again. Ian believed there was some weird malfunction with the cameras. During the day, the cameras were always being triggered, mostly by squirrels. It happened in the wee hours of the morning too when he and his wife were waking up and getting ready for the day. At night, there was nothing. Not even a single rabbit to cause the cameras to record.

Ian had spent hours on the phone with customer service checking and double checking the settings. Everything appeared fine on their end. Finally they sent someone out to make sure the equipment wasn't faulty. If she had known Ian suspected anything, she'd have risked it. She would've left the cameras on and hoped she stayed put in her bed. There was no warning until the day when Ian didn't rush out the door, but waited for the technician she didn't know was coming instead.

"Everything appears in working order," the technician said.

Claire stood in the hall near the open office door trying to be quiet as a mouse. If Ian discovered her secret, he wouldn't keep it to himself. The fight would be in full force as soon as the door closed when the guy from Safeworks left. What she wanted was a heads up. She needed to be prepared for whatever may be coming her way.

There was some various noises as things were being moved and shuffled around. "Do you still have notifications sent to your phone?"

"No," Ian said. "I turned them off because it was too much. We're not exactly in the country, but we're too rural for my phone to ding every time an animal darts through the yard."

That was news to her. Ian kept her in the dark about all of it except that the cameras were installed. She still believes he never would've mentioned it at all if she hadn't come home when she did that day to see the technician was here for herself. He claimed it was for her own good like he said about everything he did, but it didn't make her feel protected. It made her feel controlled.

"And no one is turning them off?"

"What do you mean?" Ian asked.

"The cameras. You're certain no one is turning them off and forgetting to switch them back on?"

"No one has the passwords to all of this, but me."

There was a long pause, and Claire hoped the technician was looking at her husband questionably. She had heard Ian tell him before that he was going to discuss it and explain things with his wife. If only she could see them. She wanted the guy from the security company to give him a judgmental look, but mostly she wanted to witness it.

There was a loud sigh which she guessed came from the

technician. "Alright. I'm going to uninstall and reinstall the program."

"I already did that three nights ago when I was on the phone with you guys!" Ian sounded flustered, and so far, it was the only thing to cheer Claire up a bit.

"Well, we'll try it again and hope it works this time. Otherwise the only option is to replace all the equipment."

There was more scuffling, and Claire could tell Ian was letting the technician have access to the computer. "That's more like it. That's what needs to be done."

"Don't be so quick," the technician warned him. "If the problem is on our end, then we're responsible. But if it's not, it's on you."

"What do you mean?"

"If we switch everything out, and it doesn't solve the problem, you pick up the bill for the new cameras."

That shut Ian up real quick. Claire clamped her hand over her mouth to help stifle her giggle. She could picture the look on her husband's face, and it was quite comical.

The next several minutes creeped by slowly. "There," the technician finally said. "Let's see how that works out." He also walked Ian through resetting the password just to be safe. Luckily for her, Ian always hid them in the same location.

She could hear him gathering his tools and his bag, so she hurried off to the kitchen, pretending to clean. As the two men walked to the door, she heard the technician advise him if it didn't work, he could request an audit of the command history for the account just in case someone is tampering with them.

'Shit! I didn't know that was possible.'

"Like I told you, no one else has the login information."

Ian left for work shortly after that, and Claire spent the day pacing the house trying to figure out what to do. She would have to leave the cameras on now. He was going to learn the truth one way or the other. Either he'd get the history log and see she had found the password, or he'd watch the video of her nocturnal habits whenever she had another episode.

Finally, she went back to the office and logged in. If her husband requested a history of the activity on the account, she was already busted. One more time wouldn't make a difference. She played around with the options and settings until she formulated a new plan.

Whenever she emerged from the woods, she was in the backyard. While she never remembered leaving the house, it would be safe to assume she went into the woods from the back as well. She'd leave the front cameras and the ones on the other side of the house on at night. Maybe there'd be enough critters running around after dark her husband wouldn't pay attention to the fact they were never in the backyard.

It didn't work for long. Claire caught him mumbling to himself in his office one Saturday morning. "What's wrong?" she asked, having no idea it was actually about the cameras. If she had to guess, she'd have thought he was upset over the scores of the game from last night. It hadn't been a full week yet since she altered how she manipulated the cameras.

"Nothing," Ian growled. "Just looks like I'm going to miss work again for that technician to come out."

He walked out of the office and into the kitchen, rummaging through the cabinets for a snack. "I wonder how much this is going to wind up costing me before it's over."

Claire bit her tongue. There was plenty she had to say about the new security set up, the cost involved, and what her husband could do with it all. She chose to stay quiet. Things had been good between them, really good, for a couple weeks. Each time she woke in the woods, she was filled with a longing and desire still new to her. Her husband wasn't complaining about her recently discovered sex drive either. She didn't want to destroy all of that with a fight, especially one that would get them nowhere.

'New plan,' she decided instead. *I won't turn the cameras off. I'll delete the footage when I get back in the morning.'*

It was never a guarantee she'd be back in time before Ian caught her, but it was better than nothing. So far, she had managed to get the cameras turned on before he came downstairs on the nights she went exploring in her sleep. Eventually, he'd wonder why her nighttime escapades suddenly stopped altogether. He'd probably celebrate it only to be doubly upset when one happened again.

Plus, it would work out better that way. If he was ever certain she had left the house after he went to bed, there damn well better be footage for it.

Within two weeks, he was on to her again. "Have you been tampering with the security cameras?" The question came at her out of right field over dinner one night.

"What?" She almost choked on her salad.

Ian didn't lift his eyes from his plate and continued to prepare his next bite. "Have you done anything to the settings? Primarily the recordings?" He lifted his fork to his lips without glancing at her.

Claire dropped her fork to her plate. "Ian, I barely know anything about that stuff." She stopped short of saying she doubted he'd even have told her about them at all if she had taken longer at the store that day. "How would I know what to do with them?"

He tilted his head to the side like he was considering her words while he chewed. His focus went back to his meal, slicing and collecting another bite on the tip of his fork. Then he gave a little nod to himself like he decided he was satisfied with her answer.

Pausing to talk again before bringing the fork to his mouth, he said, "It's just been very strange. There were no nightly recordings. Then only recordings on two sides of the house."

"Sounds like whatever may have been wrong worked itself out then," she said when he took his next bite.

"Maybe, but there are still nights when nothing is recorded in the backyard. Yet, there are dozens of clips from wildlife everywhere else."

'Dang it. I should've occasionally deleted the other footage too. From now on, I will,' she told herself.

"Maybe that's all there was on those nights." She tried to be as nonchalant as possible.

Nothing else was said for a few minutes, but she could tell by his demeanor it wasn't over. There was still something on his mind he hadn't figured out how to bring up yet.

Ian set down his fork and pushed his plate away. He rested his elbows on the table and rubbed his hands together. "The thing is I had something occur to me a few days ago."

"What's that?" Claire's stomach flipped, and her anxiety began to rise. She didn't like his tone and had a feeling she knew where the conversation was heading. She just didn't know how he figured it out.

"The last morning there was no activity in the backyard was

the last morning you were in one of your new rare moods."

"Rare moods?"

He folded his arms and stared directly at her. "You know exactly what I'm talking about. I couldn't stop thinking about it, so I checked the calendar at work, and it seems the last several times you've gone all nympho on me have been mornings when nothing was recorded."

"Nympho!" The word flew out of her mouth. She'd never been called anything close to that in her life, and it pissed her off hearing her own husband say it. "I don't like where you're headed with this," she said. "I don't like being accused of lying."

"No more than I don't particularly care for liars."

That was enough. She pushed away her plate and tossed her napkin on the table. As she stood to leave, he dropped one more bit of information on her.

"So I requested an activity record, or log history, whatever it's called for the account."

Claire froze in place, but only for a moment before she continued to walk away from the table. It had been long enough for Ian to notice.

"Do you want to tell me what you've been up to?" His voice followed her out of the kitchen. "Or shall I tell you what I already know and share with you how my mind has filled in the blanks?"

She ran up to the bedroom. There was no escaping this fight, but she hoped a few minutes might buy her something, some pathetic idea to help her out of this mess. She could explain turning off the cameras or deleting the footage. Ian wouldn't like it, but she had her own reasons for it. What she couldn't explain is how aroused the woods made her, and that would be the one question Ian wanted answered above the rest.

Chapter Eight

Strip Tease

Their fight lasted for days, and it wasn't finished yet. It was still there, beneath the surface. The tensions and attitude between them was at a low boil. They maintained themselves well and had prevented another blow up, but nothing had been resolved. It wouldn't take much for it to boil over again. One stressful day at work for Ian or one wrong glance at his wife, and they'd be at each other, gloves off in an instant.

There was no fix for this, for either of them. She had betrayed his trust. For weeks, she had snuck around messing with the security system. She turned the cameras on and off to fit her will.

He didn't want to hide things like that from her, but it looked like it may come to that. That's what he had shouted at her during their first confrontation after the truth came out. He might have already been doing it.

Ian never shared the new system with her willingly. There was no discussion about it before or after it was installed. When she mentioned it, he'd shrug and say it was for their safety if he said anything at all. He didn't walk her through it, show her the new cameras or explain how they worked. She was never allowed to see the footage recorded. He only mentioned nonchalantly when a squirrel or other animal had tripped the sensor. When she asked to see it, his reply was always the same. "I already deleted it."

There was no one she could discuss this with either. She had no family. The constant moving going from one home to another during her childhood, and her own issues kept all would be friends at arm's length throughout her life. She only had Ian and her therapist. Both had let her down. Ian by pushing her more than she could handle and her therapist for agreeing with him, taking his side. Claire had canceled every appointment since that day and would never go back, not to that therapist anyway.

There was too much going on at home right now. It was more than she could deal with at one time which put calling around to get set up somewhere new with a different counselor out of the question. It put her in a difficult position because now is when she could use someone to talk to the most, and she was alone.

Neither of them would budge, but it really came down to one thing. Ian wanted to know what she did in the woods at night and wouldn't accept, "I don't remember," as an answer even though it was the truth.

Claire reached her limit with it. If this was going to be the end of her marriage, the end of her life near the patch of woods which had called to her since she was a child, she was going to have fun as her world exploded around her.

Ian installed a lock on his office door. Two of them to be exact. He had the doorknobs changed to require a keyed entry plus he had a number pad added to the home alarm system just for his office which required a different pin. The only tidbit he had been forthcoming about was letting her know it would send a text to his phone every time someone tried to access the office whether the pin was successful or not. He even demonstrated it to prove to her he was being honest about it.

That night, Claire didn't retire to the bedroom with her

husband when he went to bed. Even though they were barely on speaking terms, she could tell it angered him. She never could understand why she had to drop everything to lay down with him regardless of how wide awake she was. There had been so many nights she tossed and turned for hours just to avoid an argument. Whenever she was exhausted and wanted to head to bed before him, it was laughable for her to suggest he come up with her when he wasn't ready yet.

She sat on the couch, eyes frozen to the television screen although not really watching the movie she had started. Everything about Ian repulsed her now. She didn't want to talk to him, didn't want to even look at him. When his footsteps made it to the top of the stairs and retreated down the hallway, she exhaled loudly, unaware she had been holding her breath.

Then she got mad. Her anger continued to rise the more she thought about the position he was putting her in against her will.

'What if she slept walked? What if the notification sent to his phone actually woke him from his dead sleep? Or if he happened to stir shortly afterward and see it in time? What would he do?'

Claire walked to the back of the house and looked out over the darkened yard to the trees on the edge of the property. She strained her eyes trying to see if there was anything in the woods watching her. She stretched her arms up then clasped her hands together behind her head. *'Don't be silly. There's nothing there.'*

Something had happened in those woods so many years ago. Something that still drew her to them. There was nothing there now she was certain. It did bother her the way she awoke beneath the trees feeling aroused and feeling watched. It had to stem from a dream or a past she couldn't remember which was worrisome enough. Mostly, she felt like she was healing. The woods, nature, was healing her a little at a time whenever she went back.

Ian would not ruin this for her. She wouldn't let him. If he wanted a show, which it appeared he did, she would give him one.

'But not here,' she thought, turning to walk to the front of the house. She'd lead him in a different direction and walk out the front door. The backyard and the trees that bordered it had to remain hers as long as possible. She couldn't protect it forever. The next time she woke in the woods she wouldn't be able to prevent him from narrowing down where it was she went, but she didn't have to give up that secret tonight.

Claire walked out the front door and ran out onto the lawn. She ran from one side of the house to the other, back and forth, triggering as many cameras out front as she could. She yelled at them even though she knew they didn't record sound. Well, as far as she knew, they didn't. It's hard to say what other changes Ian had made without updating her. It made her hope they picked up every word she had to say.

"Is this what you want?" She screamed at the camera near the edge of her porch.

In the middle of the lawn where at least two cameras would pick up on her movement, she began to dance as seductively as possible. She hummed a popular club song from her college days, and let her hands roam over her body while she swayed to the beat.

She hadn't got ready for bed yet, so she was still in an oversized tee-shirt and cutoff blue jean shorts. It wasn't the sexiest outfit by any means, but she worked it as well as she could.

Claire unbuttoned her shorts and turned around showing the cameras a great view of her backside. She shimmied and sashayed the shorts down her legs and kicked them away. Then she used her shirt to tease the cameras by lifting it and pulling it to the sides to flash brief images of her panties.

"I hope you like what you see, Ian! It may be the last time you get a peek."

Her impromptu strip tease continued until she grew tired of it. She lifted the shirt off over head throwing it aside. She reached behind her back and unfastened her bra, letting it slide off her arms and drop to the ground near her feet. She firmly squeezed her breasts with her hands for a couple minutes, adding to her show.

Turning her back to the house once again, she wiggled her way out of her panties and stepped out of them. Slowly she circled until she faced the porch with one arm covering her breasts and the other protecting her sweet mound from view. Her mouth dropped open and her eyes widened as if she were shocked to find herself on the lawn completely naked.

"That's what you think happens, isn't it? You believe I'm out here slutting around for anyone who happens to stumble upon me when I'm asleep."

One by one she let her arms drop then raised them above her head. She spread her feet apart until she was fully exposed to the cameras and did a slow three-sixty turn to make sure Ian saw everything easily. Then she walked back to the porch, flipping off the cameras with both hands as she went.

Claire dropped onto the wicker rattan on the side of the porch and pulled the throw blanket draped over the back onto her body. This is where she would sleep tonight. In the morning, there would be hell to pay, but she was going to enjoy a night of fresh air and peace first.

She had a lot on her mind and tossed and turned, trying to get comfortable while thinking things over. It might be a good thing she was on the outs with her therapist. No progress had been made for quite a long time. Maybe it was time to see someone else, to get a fresh opinion from someone more objective than the therapist she was seeing. It may even be time to try hypnosis again.

It had never worked out well in the past, but she hadn't been too open to the experience. She was afraid of finding out the truth as much as she wanted to know what it was. With a new counselor and a new plan of action which included her wanting to put the past behind her once and for all, it might work this time.

As for Ian, she wasn't sure what she was going to do. She couldn't forgive him for a lot of this. It wasn't entirely his fault, and she knew it. They weren't a good match. It was time they both admitted that fact. It wouldn't be easy, not for her at least, but they needed to go their separate ways. He needed a woman he could control, and she needed a man who understood protecting her included keeping her mental health safe as well.

She wouldn't delve into that in the morning. He'd be pissed over tonight, and their fighting would start afresh. For the next few days, she'd be on her best behavior. She'd let the dust settle, and let things return as normal as possible. In the meantime, she'd start looking for a job and an apartment. Even if she got the house in the divorce, she'd have to sell it. There's no way she could stay on top of the mortgage.

It saddened her, but not because she didn't want to lose Ian. It would be hard to start over again. Ian had his faults. He had a long list of them, but he'd been more accepting of her past and her sleep walking than anyone she'd ever met. If it didn't work out with him, she had serious doubts it would work with anyone.

As she lay there slowly drifting off, she wondered if it wasn't her anger talking. She had worked herself up again by putting on a show, trying to evoke her husband's wrath. Maybe after a good night's sleep, things would seem different. She might not be so ready to give up on him in the morning. The new counselor was the first step before making massive decisions which would affect the rest of her life.

Chapter Nine

The Kiss

Claire woke up several moments before she opened her eyes. It was a perplexing state between consciousness and sleep where she couldn't remember where she was or what had happened. Between the dream of a handsome stranger rescuing her and the breeze blowing through her hair, she felt the confusion claw at her mind.

Then it all came flooding back to her. She had slept on the porch in the nude because she couldn't stand her husband any longer. She decided to do whatever she could to push his buttons.

'*But...*' Her fingertips flew to her lips almost expecting to touch someone else. The crushing weight of the kiss was still on them. As she became more and more awake, she was positive it hadn't been part of a dream. It was real. Ian wouldn't reward her with such a sweet awakening after how she behaved last night.

Claire opened her eyes and swiftly realized it wasn't Ian. She didn't know whose lips had woken her that morning, but they didn't belong to her husband. She watched the early morning light flow through the branches of the trees, dripping down to cascade over her. The more awake she became the more her memories rushed back.

She jumped to her feet surprised to see she was in her tee-shirt. The other clothes she had stripped off last night lay beside her, and she grabbed for them. Claire hurried as fast as she could while trying to get dressed as she made her way out of the trees.

Once inside her house, she waited for Ian. He was awake by now and probably in the shower. He would've seen the text notifications by now though.

'Apparently, a shower takes priority over looking for his wife.'

Maybe he hadn't gone that far through the video clips sent to his phone. There would've been plenty from her antics on the lawn last night. He might not know yet she had slept in the woods again. Either way, there would be a fight when he came downstairs, and he would claim this last sleep walking episode as proof the cameras were warranted.

She looked down the hall toward the rear of the house. In her hurry to get home, she had come through the backyard. It narrowed down the location of where she had been. She had always told Ian it was a different spot within the woods where she'd awaken. From the moment the lie slipped her lips the first time, she hadn't understood why she didn't tell the truth about it. Now, she had a better understanding. It was hers and needed to stay hers alone, even if she didn't grasp why she felt that way.

Her eyes fell on the locked office door. There was nothing she could do about it. Ian would see she had been in the back part of the woods closer to the creek. It'd be fine this time, but in the future, she would need to walk inside the tree line until she was closer to the house before emerging.

There was movement above her, and she heard his footsteps walk down the hall toward the stairs. Claire scurried back to the kitchen to make coffee. If he didn't yet know she had sleep walked, she could save that part of the fight until tonight.

"Good morning," Ian said, kissing her on top of the head. "How did you sleep?"

This was odd. She expected him to tear into her about her strip tease. "Great," she said quietly.

"That didn't sound convincing," he laughed. "Lots of footage from the cameras last night."

"Oh?" This was it. She took a deep breath, waiting for his tone to become angry.

"Yeah," he sounded concerned. "I wasn't too sure the cameras were working at first. Most of the clips didn't show anything."

Claire was willing to keep up the charade as long as he was. "Maybe something small. Like a field mouse?" she shrugged. *It's not like I would know how powerful the cameras are and what they can pick up.*'

"Hmm maybe." He didn't sound convinced. "But the wolf certainly caught my attention."

"Wolf?" Claire's head snapped around to him from the pineapple she was slicing to have with their breakfast. "Are you serious? A wolf?"

Ian nodded and pulled out his phone. He touched the screen a few times then showed it to her. The first video caught on the cameras she was allowed to see was a tan colored wolf who walked up almost to the bottom step of the porch.

"Scary, isn't it?" he asked. "There's a few more of the wolf on the lawn not doing much, but this was the closest he got."

Claire continued preparing breakfast waiting for Ian to say something else. It was all building up to it. That angle didn't show her sleeping on the rattan, but there had to be another video which did. Not only had she made an ass of herself dancing on the lawn and sleeping on the porch until her episode, but a wolf came by to investigate her. There was no choice but to cede the fight as soon as it began.

Only Ian never said another word about the cameras, the videos, or any of it. She ate her breakfast in silence. He had to be waiting for her to volunteer the information or slip up, saying something that gave her away. He wouldn't wait forever. Eventually, the argument would begin with or without her help.

"I didn't know there were wolves in this area." Claire finally spoke up bringing the topic back around. It would help get everything off his chest quicker.

Ian looked up from his plate at her like he forgot she was in the room. "Me either. Well, there used to be. I knew that much, but it's been years, at least a decade, since one has been spotted."

Still nothing about what she did and where she was last night. "I guess we'll have to be more careful then."

He nodded and stood up. "Definitely. I'm going to call it in today to the department of wildlife or whoever handles things like this. I'll let you know if they say they're coming by."

Ian walked over and put one arm around his wife and pulled her to him. "I've got to head to work. Just be safe. You know I worry. They aren't nocturnal creatures. It'd make me feel better if you promised to check around through the windows before leaving the house."

"I promise," Claire said. He was leaving without a cross word. Something really was wrong with the system.

After a quick kiss, Ian left the house, and Claire breathed a large sigh of relief. She sat at the table in shock for several minutes. It could still be buried notifications. The blowup could come later tonight, but how she managed to get through the morning without a fight came as a total shock.

She picked up the dishes and carried them to the sink to load in the dishwasher. Ian's kiss was routine. It had no more effect than a handshake. But, it made her think of the one left on her lips right before she woke hours earlier. That kiss had meant something. It had been full of passion and lust. Her lips still tingled from thinking about it.

After loading the dishwasher, she wiped down the table and the sink. She didn't have plans for the day and wondered what she'd spend it doing. The idea of searching for a job and an apartment still danced around in her head, but she was tired. Every night she slept in the woods left her exhausted the next day like she hadn't slept much at all.

Today was no different in that regard, but it wasn't anywhere like the others either. The kiss that was on her lips when she awoke still haunted her. The memory of it was all but gone, but the way it made her feel hadn't diminished one bit. Just thinking about it made her pulse thump hard in her clit and made her legs weak. The desire it stirred deep inside flowed through her veins and reached every part of her body. Each visit to the woods over the last several weeks left her in a higher and higher spell of dizzying sexual excitement.

Thanks to Ian being open for once, there was so much more to the mystery. As far as she knew, Ian still hadn't seen any surveillance clips with her as the star. It seemed impossible, but the lack of any accusations and anger this morning was all the proof she needed. Her only explanation was he got tired of the sheer number of clips and deleted them without looking at each one. If that was the case, she'd been extremely lucky and wouldn't do something as juvenile as she did last night again.

Then there was the wolf which came close to the porch and

seemed to watch her sleep. It had to mean something too.

'That's absurd.'

Even as she thought it, she knew better. There was something almost familiar about the wolf which sounded even more ridiculous. She didn't see it as a creature capable of causing great harm which it absolutely could, and she was well aware of it. To her, it was loving and nurturing. It watched over her for protection not to harm. Claire wouldn't be able to explain how she knew that no matter how hard she tried, but she'd swear on anything it was the truth.

If the wolf watched her sleeping on the porch, it was very possible it had come across her in the woods too. That's probably why it didn't scare her to see the video on Ian's phone. She had no memories of it, but she must've sensed it subconsciously somehow.

Claire was walking through the mud room to head out back before she was aware of what she was doing. The draw to the woods was strong today. It called to her louder and more insistent than it ever had. Every ounce of what little energy she had was spent keeping her feet from going down the steps and running to the trees.

She forced herself to go back inside, to shower and change. She needed to rest. Sleep walking was akin to pulling an all nighter in how drained it left her the next day. There were other tasks on her list too. She needed to decide once and for all if she was going to stay in this lackluster marriage or find a way to escape. There was still time for that later, and it might not be today when she made up her mind for good.

Right now, she needed sleep. Tonight, she had some very important business to tend to which would require a lot of strength.

Chapter Ten

Her Guardian

When Ian went to bed, she slipped out. Her mind had been made up shortly after he left for work that morning, but it was reinforced throughout the day. She couldn't get the woods out of her mind. They called to her like some supernatural force which captivated her, made her forget all logic, and throw caution to the wind because she had to know. Whenever it happened, her lips tingled with the memory of the kiss.

This was something she felt compelled to do. Her episodes had always been random. Sometimes she went months without one, and then she'd wake in the woods five times in a few weeks. This was different somehow. She couldn't put it into words, but she felt it.

Claire didn't know what to expect when she went to the woods while she was still awake. She had made up her mind it was going to be her litmus test. If nothing happened, she'd step up her therapy, try to heal the past trauma and unlock the memories of it to do so. But, if anything happened, it would be time to move on. She was hoping the woods might spark a feeling or a clue, but she wasn't about to hold her breath. The last thing she thought she'd find was Dylan.

She entered the woods near the end of the backyard around where she usually emerged. Her feet remembered the way, carrying her through the trees with little effort to wonder where. It wasn't long before she came upon the beautiful tall tree she'd woken underneath on so many mornings. There she sat, waiting, hoping, but not knowing for what.

An hour passed, and she didn't move from her spot. There was something frightening about being alone in the woods after dark fall. Every noise was a potential threat, but it calmed her too. Something told her she was safe here; she was more protected in this exact spot than anywhere else.

There was a noise to her left. Something rather large was making its way through the underbrush toward her. Claire's heart beat faster, but it was from excitement rather than terror. She slowly moved her head and could barely make out the outline of a tan wolf emerging from the growth in the moon light shining through the trees.

Claire looked down at her feet. Her brain sounded alarms and scrambled the archives of everything she ever learned in school or articles she might've read about how to survive a wolf attack, but her heart told her this was a friend.

"You came," a voice said softly to her.

She looked up, but didn't see anyone. The wolf was no longer nearby as well. Then a man stepped from behind a tree, pulling a shirt over his head. Claire sucked her breath between her teeth, and whispered, "Dylan."

The man sat across from her, tucking his legs beneath his body. Her eyes adjusted, and she could see him clearly. His disheveled dark brown hair framed his face, and his brown eyes bored into hers. She lifted her hand, mesmerized, being pulled like a magnet to touch his square jawline, but she resisted.

"I had begun to worry you wouldn't show."

"You'd been through a lot. It would be hard for you to process everything, so I thought it'd help."

"How can you do that? You can't just erase memories in someone."

Dylan cracked his neck from side to side. "Let me explain."

The story he wove would've sounded absurd to her last week, maybe even earlier that day, but somehow she knew every word was true. Everything he told her felt like a reminder not a new lesson.

He was a wolf. His people had roamed this area for generations. They happened to be nearby that night which is how he came to rescue her. His kind were mated. They're matches are controlled by their genes, not by choice, but his mate had died which left him free to choose a new mate. He simply didn't have the heart to do so, feeling like he deserved to be alone since he couldn't save her when she had her accident.

Feeling the way he did and finding a child in need of help, he bonded with Claire. In that way, he could order her to forget.

"Bonded?" Claire's hand immediately flew to her chest to shield her body. She feared what meaning might be attached to that word.

Dylan chuckled and sat upright. "Nothing like that. I simply chose you."

"What does that mean exactly?"

He sighed and stretched his arms in front of him. "Typically, it means I met a woman without a mate, fell in love, and we decided for ourselves to be mated."

"But?"

"But instead I gave up the chance of finding a mate to protect you from what happened. You are my only priority in life and have been since I met you as a child."

"That's why I'm called to the woods?"

He stood up and walked a few feet away. With his back to her, he said, "Yes. I wanted to check on you. I'd come to the spot where we bonded and call for you."

"It's been increasing." Claire said the words out loud wondering if there was a reason for it.

Dylan walked back to her and pulled her up to him. "My people are leaving. The land is becoming too developed to support our... nocturnal outings. I wanted to say goodbye. Then..."

She waited, but he didn't continue. "Then what? What is it you didn't expect to happen?"

He leaned his face in until their mouths nearly touched. "Then you told me you loved me."

Claire was entranced and almost kissed him then she stepped back. "Because of the bond."

"No," he shook his head, stepping toward her and closing the space between them again. "You're not a wolf. You can't bond to me."

His lips grazed hers, and she gasped. Dylan looked into her eyes for a moment before pressing down hard on her mouth and pulling her body tightly to him.

There was no gorgeous house nearby loaded with cameras. There was no Ian. There was no marriage. There was only Dylan, the man her heart agreed loved him completely even if her mind still struggled with organizing the newly found memories.

"Tonight's the last night," he whispered. "We leave tomorrow. It's up to you to come or not."

Claire intertwined her fingers behind his head and pulled

his lips back to hers. He wrapped one arm around her waist and lowered her to the ground. He stripped his clothes off and lowered himself on top of her, spreading her legs apart with his knee.

"Have we...?" she wanted to know.

"No," he said. "I couldn't. Not until I unlocked your memories. I couldn't take advantage of you like that and send you home in the morning wondering what happened."

"But we've kissed?"

In the darkness, she could see his grin. "Yes. The last few times you were here, and stopping at a kiss was the hardest thing I've ever done."

His mouth kissed hers gently then traveled down her neck and along the top of her breasts. He lifted her nightgown up until her midsection was exposed, and he continued the trail of kisses down until he reached her inner thigh.

The sensations rocking through her core were similar to what she experienced with Ian in the kitchen, but different. This time her body reacted to Dylan easily instead of relying on being previously turned on.

His head disappeared between her legs, and she felt his tongue enter her labyrinth. Moans escaped her throat easily. He toyed with her clit with his finger while his tongue worked its magic in her tunnel. Claire's back arched, and she grabbed the back of his head, thrusting into his face.

In a few minutes, she was cumming. Her juices flowed over his mouth and down his chin. Dylan lifted his head up and watched her, smiling.

"I'm coming," she said.

Dylan laughed. "I think you already did."

"No," she shook her head breathlessly. "Tomorrow. I'm coming with you."

Coming Soon

Kindle Vella:
Deadly Sins: Greed

Kindle:
Family Secrets #5

More by Darling Coxx

The Nanny Diaries Series

ALL FIVE INSTALLMENTS of this series are now available! Follow the journey of five young women trying to make their way in the world who have taken jobs as live-in nannies. These books are their diaries. Read about the adventures they had taking care of their own needs. Check them out if you dare! Darling Coxx's writing always scratches the itch you can't reach on your own.

Family Secrets Series

All five installments of this series are now available! Follow five pseudo taboo couplings. They might not be blood related, but they are a little close for some people's comfort.

Supernatural Erotica
True Love's Kiss

CLAIRE WAS HAUNTED by a past she couldn't remember. Her sleepwalking always led her to the same area of the woods like it called to her, but she'd wake up with no memory of going there or the time that passed. It led to problems in her marriage and left her with so many questions. That was all about to change. The one man who held the answers she sought and held a power over her she didn't understand was about to reveal himself.

Deadly Sins
Pride

SEVEN DEADLY SINS; seven highly erotic stories. Season one covers Pride. Stacey should be a little humbler when dealing with the people around her. She doesn't know who she's actually dealing with. After inheriting her late husband's business, she's enjoying living off the results of his hard work. The new and much younger man in her life stands poised to take it all from her.

About the Author

Darling Coxx is a seasoned writer who has been featured in many major publications under her given name. Taking a break from interviews and personal experience pieces, she is trying her hand at short novellas in the same genre she's been working in for most of her life.

Her adult entertainment career began while working as the manager of an adult store. It is her favorite position of any she's held, before or since. It was there where she made the contacts that allowed her to venture into the world of adult entertainment both in her own writing as well as producing a few pieces of her own.

Please feel free to reach out to her at DarlingCoxx@gmail.com. Follow her on Instagram @DarlingCoxx to stay updated on future publications.